DARK'S G

A Boy's Journey
From Fear To Appreciation

Once upon a time, in a world full of light,
lived a being named Dark, a mysterious creature of the night.
He roamed the world, with the moon as his guide,
bringing the shadows and the stars to shine bright.

Dark set the stage for the night sky's display,
with constellations and planets, on a cosmic array.
He created the perfect conditions, for the stars to twinkle,
and the galaxies to shine, in a cosmic wrinkle.

But not everyone appreciated Dark's handiwork,
many shied away from him, and preferred to lurk.
He was sad, he had no friends to play,
all because the people thought he was scary and grey.

One night, as Dark wandered all alone,
he stumbled upon a small house, made of stone.
He saw a young boy named Eloy, lying in his bed,
trembling and sweating, with fear in his head.

Dark sensed Eloy's fear of the night,
so he decided to reach out and make things right.
He crept into the room, with a friendly smile,
hoping he would give him a chance, for a little while

Eloy was startled, as Dark came into view,
Who are you? What do you want? Please don't hurt me, I beg you."
"I'm Dark, I'm here to show you the beauty of the night,
and guide you on a journey of wonder and delight."

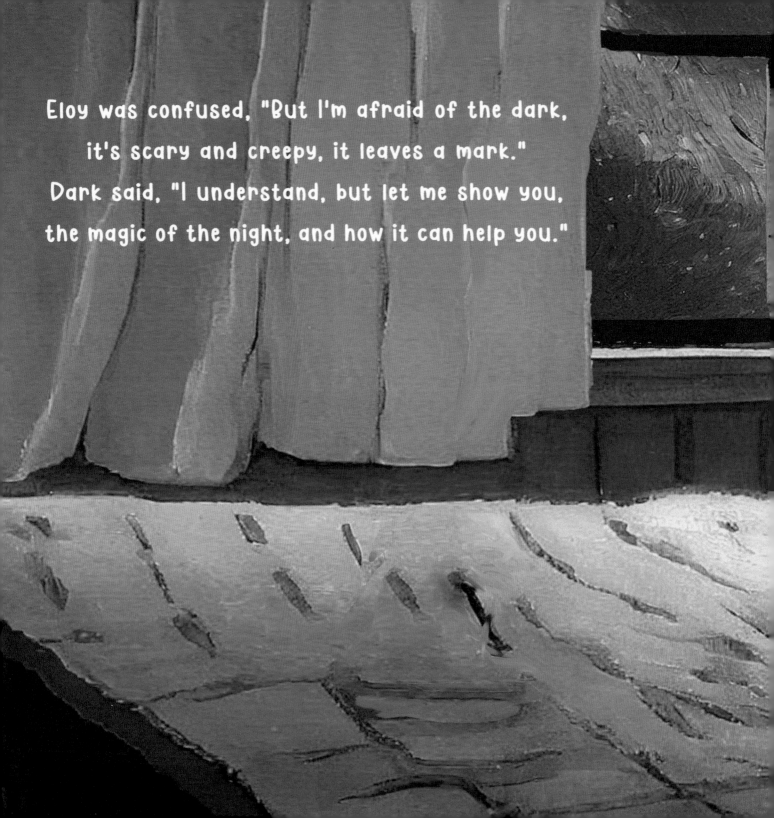

Eloy was confused, "But I'm afraid of the dark,
it's scary and creepy, it leaves a mark."
Dark said, "I understand, but let me show you,
the magic of the night, and how it can help you."

Eloy was hesitant, but he decided to trust,

Dark's gentle words, and his kind touch.

He showed him the stars, shining bright and bold,

and Eloy was amazed, by the stories they told.

Dark showed him, how the night sky can inspire,
and how it can help imagination set the mind on fire.
He taught Eloy how to find patterns in the stars,
and how to let his mind wander, free from earthly bars.

Eloy saw the Milky Way, a galaxy grand,
and the shooting stars, that crossed the land.
He realized, that Dark wasn't so scary,
it was a canvas, for the mind to be merry.

Eloy was in awe, as he took in the sight,
of the dark canvas, full of twinkling light.
He then turned to Dark and said with surprise,
"I never knew you could be so nice."

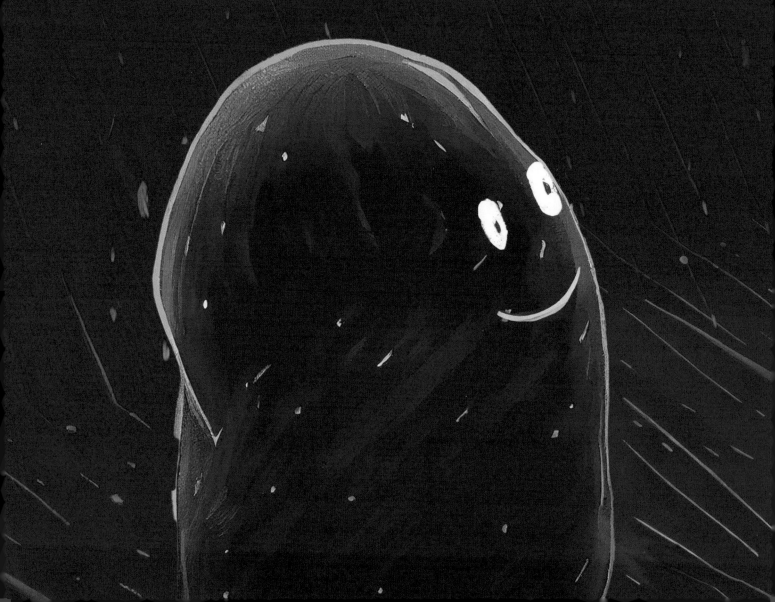

Dark smiled and said, "I'm glad you see,
the beauty in me, that's plain to me."
He then added, "I'm happy you find peace,
with me by your side, your fears will cease."

Dark explained how he can help with sleep,
and how he's necessary for our bodies to keep.
He spoke of how he can improve mood,
and help with the circadian rhythm, making one feel good.

Dark spoke of how he brings magic to slumber,
make dreams sweet and peaceful, free of any blunder.
And help to regulate the body's internal clock,
allowing for better sleep and a feeling of being on top.

Eloy was in awe of all the secrets Dark had concealed,
and realized that Dark was a treasure to be revealed.
He then pleaded, "Please stay by my side,
protect me as I sleep, be my guide."

Dark happily agreed to stay with Eloy,
to guide him through the night, and bring him joy.
From that day on, Eloy felt safe and sound,
with Dark by his side, no longer feeling bound.

Printed in Great Britain
by Amazon